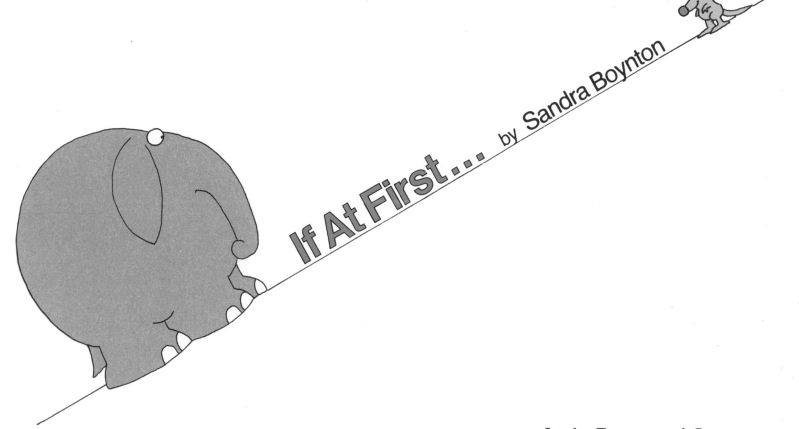

If At First... by Sandra Boynton

Little, Brown and Company
BOSTON   TORONTO

IF AT FIRST by Sandra Boynton
from an idea by James McEwan

Library of Congress Cataloging in Publication Data

Boynton, Sandra.
  If at first . . .

  SUMMARY: A determined mouse tries, tries, and tries again to move a lazy elephant up a hill.
  [1. Mice—Fiction 2. Elephants—Fiction]
I. McEwan, James. II. Title
PZ7.B6968If   [E]   79-24310
ISBN 0-316-10487-6
ISBN 0-316-10486-8 pbk.

HOR

*Published simultaneously in Canada
by Little, Brown & Company (Canada) Limited*

PRINTED IN THE UNITED STATES OF AMERICA

For Laurie

If at first

you don't succeed,

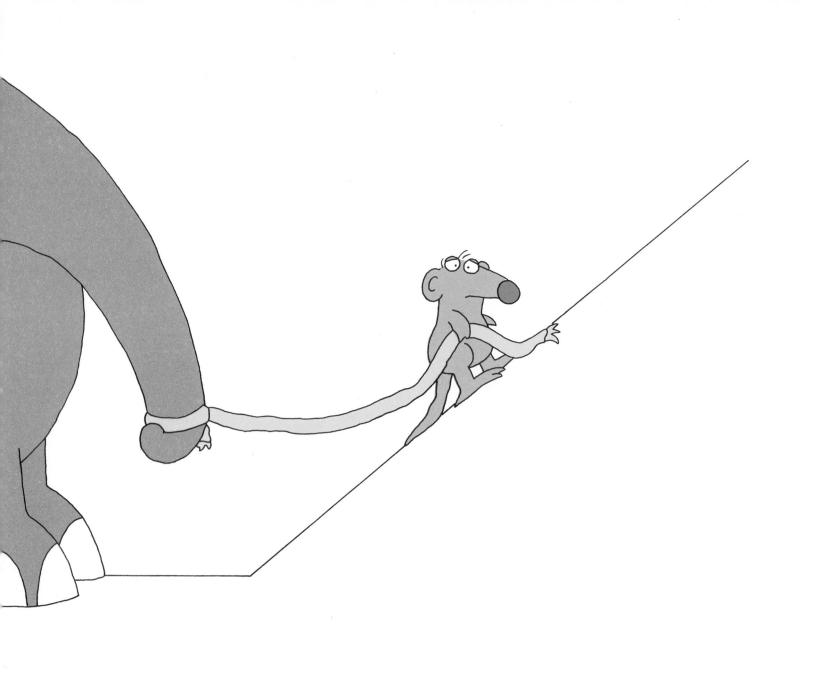

try,

try,

try,

"Try, try, try!"

(Don't cry, cry, cry.)

sigh . . .

try,

try,

try,

try

again.